Alena Change$ Everything

Written by: James Alvarez   Illustrated by: Ghyvari Gisymar

This Book Belongs To :

____

"Grandma Gloria and Grandpa Juan are here!!!"

"Good morning, my little mijos!"
"Good morning, Grandma!"
WELCOME

"You three know I love you, right? I would like for you to know just how much I love you."

"Felix, mijo, hand me my purse."

"Mom, what are you doing?"

"I want to give money to my three beautiful babies."

"Mom, you need to stop doing that. They have to earn it."

"Mom, the kids need to learn how to use money..."

"Kids, you can keep the ten dollars, but I will challenge you to make the most of it!"

"Ooh, we love challenges!"

"I love that idea! Yes, I will be back in three days and see what you all come up with."

"Come on, let's go plan what to do with our money."

"Jaime, what are you going to do with your money?"
"I will use it to buy candy and ice cream!"

"Yup!
All of it!"
"You will spend all
ten dollars on candies
and ice cream?!"

"What about you, Sara? What are you going to do with your ten dollars?" Alena asked.
Sara replied, "I am going to put it somewhere safe and save it!"

"What are you going to do with your ten dollars, Alena!"

FLOUR
"I will use the money
to buy eggs, flour, and
frosting to make more
money with cupcakes."

"That sounds like a lot of work, Alena.
What if your cupcakes don't sell?"

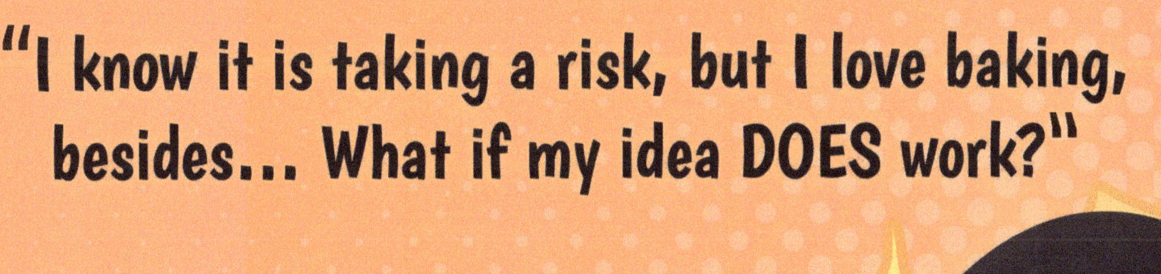

"I know it is taking a risk, but I love baking, besides... What if my idea DOES work?"

"I have chocolates to buy!"
"Where are you going, Jaime?"

"Well, I better go find a special place to hide my money."

"This is the best idea ever!!!"

"Where should I hide my money?"

"This would be a good place... maybe not."

"This will be a good place...
Okay, maybe not here either."

"This will be the perfect spot. No one will look here!"

CAKE MIX
BUTTER
EGGS
MILK
FROSTING

"First, I will make the batter and bake them in the oven."

"Then, I will build my cupcake stand
while they cool."

"Finally, I will frost all the cupcakes once they've cooled."
SPARKL

"Oh, these look delicious.
I will take three cupcakes, please."
CUPCAKE!
Sale

"I can't believe it worked; I sold all my cupcakes!"

SOLD OUT

"I'm back! Where are you, my little babies?!"

"What's wrong, Jaime? Are you sick?"

"My stomach hurts, Grandma. I think I ate too much chocolate."

"Well, I think we know how Jaime spent his money.
What did you girls do with yours?"

"I found the safest place in my room, under my...
Oh, it's a secret, but I have all ten dollars!
I saved it, Grandma!"

"That's great,
mija."

"I used my money to buy all the ingredients and had a cupcake sale! I made thirty-three dollars and seventy-five cents!"

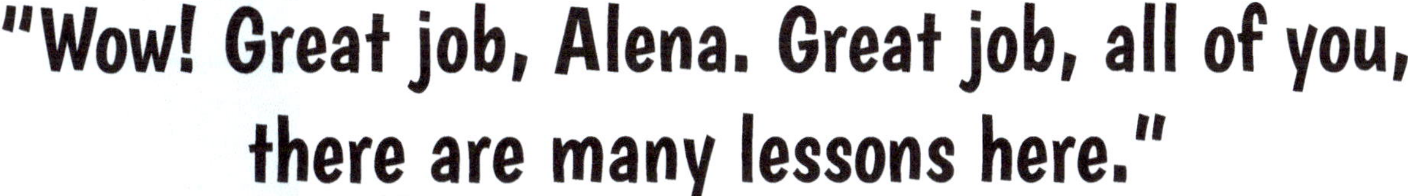

"Wow! Great job, Alena. Great job, all of you,
there are many lessons here."

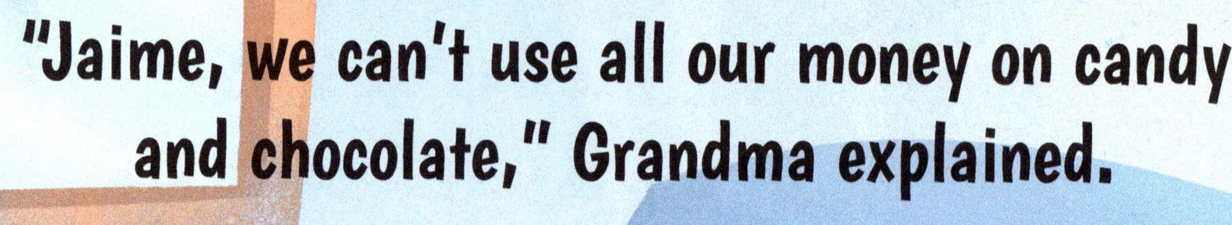

"Jaime, we can't use all our money on candy and chocolate," Grandma explained.

"Sara, saving your money is a great idea, but it doesn't make you more," said Grandma.

"Alena, you learned the lesson of reinvestment. You took your money and used it to creatively make more."

"You each get ten more dollars. I will return in three more days to see how you've reinvested it."

ABOUT THE AUTHOR

James Alvarez is passionate about empowering young readers to make smart financial choices—a passion rooted in his own upbringing in a challenging environment. He knows firsthand how financial knowledge can change lives, and he's on a mission to share that life-changing power with the next generation.

A seasoned senior leader with expertise in business management and supply chain operations, James combines professional excellence with a heart for education. He holds a Master's degree in Business Administration and is a proud first-generation college graduate, proving that hard work and perseverance can turn dreams into reality.

Through *Alena Changes Everything*, James brings practical money lessons to life, inspiring children to dream big, embrace education, and believe in their ability to achieve—no matter their background.

James believes every child deserves the tools to build the life they dream of—and it starts with one simple lesson.

9 781955 509152